SANTA ANA PUBLIC LIBRARY BG

10833765

ALADDIN
AND THE ENCHANTED LAMP

SANTA ANA PUBLIC LIBRARY

J
398.2
MAY

015.95

ALADDIN
AND THE ENCHANTED LAMP

AS TOLD BY MARIANNA MAYER
ILLUSTRATED BY GERALD McDERMOTT

MACMILLAN PUBLISHING COMPANY
New York
COLLIER MACMILLAN PUBLISHERS
London

Text copyright © 1985 by Marianna Mayer
Illustrations copyright © 1985 by Gerald McDermott

*All rights reserved. No part of this book may be reproduced
or transmitted in any form or by any means, electronic or
mechanical, including photocopying, recording or by any
information storage and retrieval system, without
permission in writing from the Publisher.*

Macmillan Publishing Company
866 Third Avenue, New York, N.Y. 10022
Collier Macmillan Canada, Inc.

Printed in the United States of America

10   9   8   7   6   5   4   3   2   1

Library of Congress Cataloging in Publication Data

Mayer, Marianna.
Aladdin and the enchanted lamp.

*Summary: Retells the adventures of Aladdin who, with
the help of a genie from a magic lamp, outwits an
evil sorcerer and wins the hand of a beautiful princess.*
*[1. Fairy tales.   2. Folklore, Arab]   I. McDermott,
Gerald, ill.   II. Aladdin.   III. Title.*
PZ8.M4514Al   1985   398.2'2   85-4894
ISBN 0-02-765360-9

B 6

For Sesyle Joslin and Alexandra Hine

The story of Aladdin has come to be regarded as part of the *Thousand and One Nights* (perhaps better known as the *Arabian Nights*). For centuries, together and separately, both have been considered universal classics. The *Nights*, a collection of fewer than two hundred folktales, owes its origin to three distinct cultures: Indian, Persian and Arab. The original core of the *Nights* sprang from a lost Persian book of fairy tales called *A Thousand Legends*, translated into Arabic about A.D. 850. In the course of time some stories have been lost while others were added, mainly from Baghdad and Cairo.

The *Nights* was first introduced to the Western world by Jean Antoine Galland, a gifted French storyteller and professor of Arabic. Between 1704 and 1717 Galland translated and published his collection in twelve volumes. It was so popular in France that almost at once the *Nights* was translated into several other European languages, including English. Galland supplemented his material with tales told to him by a Syrian friend and scholar. We have them to thank for including Aladdin's story in the collection.

The origins of *Aladdin and the Enchanted Lamp* are far more mysterious, for no one is absolutely certain of its earliest date or precise source. A Baghdad manuscript dated 1703 was discovered, and, though it was subsequently lost, there is a copy in the Bibliothèque Nationale in Paris.

With this history it may seem strange that the story of Aladdin, not really part of the earlier collection, should by the sheer force of its power become synonymous with the *Nights*. Indeed, it is the best-known tale in the collection. Told and retold for so many generations all over the world, it is often considered the best-known story ever written.

Marianna Mayer

ALADDIN
AND THE ENCHANTED LAMP

When he saw Aladdin, he smiled to himself, saying, "Yes, this is the very boy I seek."

*L*ong ago, there lived a poor tailor who had one child, named Aladdin. So great was the father's love for the boy that no trade seemed good enough for Aladdin. Indeed, in those days a poor tradesman had no chance whatever of raising his son to any station in life higher than his own. Yet the tailor was a free man and not a slave. He worked hard and long at his trade and was able, with great effort, to allow Aladdin to pass the time in any idle pursuit that amused him.

Despite his wife's admonitions, the tailor persisted in overwork that led to his falling seriously ill. Alas, he never recovered and soon died, leaving his wife and son to grieve for him in poverty. Since Aladdin had no skills, his mother sold the little tailor shop and took up cotton spinning to support herself and her son.

Years of hardship passed until one day, when Aladdin was about fifteen years old, his luck changed abruptly. A Moroccan stranger arrived in the city. Well versed in astrology, the man was a powerful sorcerer capable of hurling the sun out of the sky if he wished. His study of the stars had sent him in search of a particular boy. When he saw Aladdin, he smiled to himself, saying, "Yes, this is the very boy I seek."

Before approaching Aladdin, the sorcerer watched him in secret, making cautious inquiries into the boy's background. Then, convinced he need learn no more, the sorcerer had only to choose his moment. One day at last, he made his move. As Aladdin passed along a busy street, the sorcerer stopped him and said, "Excuse me, my boy. Are you Ali the tailor's son?"

"I am," answered Aladdin, "but my father has been dead a long time. Did you know him?"

Choking back false tears, the sorcerer reached for Aladdin and embraced him. Covering the startled boy with kisses, he said, "Oh, I am too late. My heart is surely breaking."

This great show of emotion bewildered Aladdin. Gently, he pulled himself free of the stranger and asked, "Sir, why do you weep? Were you a friend of my father's?"

"A friend!" said the sorcerer as he eyed Aladdin through a stream of tears. "More than a friend, my boy. But how could you know this? When I left, your father was not even married. Nephew, he was my own dear brother! Just now, when I chanced to see you pass, I knew instantly by your striking resemblance to him that you must be his son." Reaching into his robes, the sorcerer took from his pocket ten gold coins and handed them to the boy. "Here, take these coins. Only tell me where you live, so that I may come to you and your mother tonight to pay my respects. There is so much I wish to share with you both."

Aladdin took the coins; it was more gold than he had ever seen. He quickly told his new-found uncle where he lived and then bade him farewell till evening.

Filled with the good news, Aladdin burst through the door of his home, shouting for his mother. No sooner did she hear the story than she took the coins and hurried to the market to buy meat and fruit, wine and other delicacies for a lavish dinner.

When the meal was almost ready, there was a sharp knock at the door. Aladdin proudly led his uncle in and presented him to his mother. The sorcerer embraced her as he had Aladdin. "At last we meet, my dear sister-in-law. Tell me, after all these years, are you surprised to learn that your husband had a brother?"

The poor woman couldn't help but be taken in by the sorcerer's distinguished bearing and worldly charm. If she had any doubts about him, they soon faded from her mind. "My husband did speak of a brother but told me he was dead."

"Alas, my silence for all these years must have led him to believe I was dead. I have been remiss in my family duties—you needn't reproach me, for I know it," said the sorcerer. He let his eyes fill with tears as he took hold of her hand. "Believe me, I have paid dearly. Today, when I learned from Aladdin of my brother's untimely death, I thought my heart would break into a thousand and one pieces. If only I had come back in time."

The sorcerer's speech moved Aladdin's mother deeply, and she tried to comfort him. "There, there, it cannot be helped. You mustn't blame yourself. Please come and sit down. We are so happy to have you with us at last."

During the meal, the sorcerer talked of his travels and gave his reasons for seeking his brother out. Aladdin and his mother listened in awe, completely taken in by the sorcerer's colorful speeches and dramatic gestures. They felt something strange, perhaps even evil about him, but they dismissed it as nothing more than his worldliness. He talked rapidly as they ate, his odd, darting eyes leaping from mother to son like those of a serpent while the ghost of a smile flickered on his bloodless lips.

"After forty years of wandering, I began to think often of my own country," the sorcerer said with a heavy sigh. "Then one day, I was seized with a powerful memory of my beloved brother. So vivid was it that when I came to myself I thought, *Perhaps he is in need and would welcome my help.*" The sorcerer paused and studied his hosts, wondering if they had by now come to trust him.

He needn't have wondered, for they believed in him completely. Had they glimpsed, even for a brief moment, what really was in his mind, they would have fallen back in horror. But no lucky insight was to dawn on them that evening to foil the sorcerer's plans. Unfortunately, sometimes the dishonest have an advantage over the innocent.

The sorcerer continued, "I am a wealthy man with no family other than you and Aladdin. It would give me the greatest pleasure if you would allow me to help you both. Should you agree, I only ask that I may be permitted to make Aladdin my heir."

Aladdin's mother was filled with humble gratitude at these generous offers. "How can we refuse, brother-in-law? Your arrival is like a miracle."

"Then, my dear, leave everything to me," said the sorcerer as he stroked his black beard. Turning his eyes on Aladdin, he said, "Now, my son, for from this day forward I shall think of you as my son, what are your plans for the future? You need only tell me, and I will make everything possible for you."

Aladdin was embarrassed, for he had no plans or prospects of any kind. Seeing his distress, his mother answered for him and told the sorcerer that so far Aladdin had no profession.

"Then we must find him one," concluded the sorcerer. "My son, is there something you think you would like to do? I will have you educated at whatever trade you choose so that when you are a man you will want for nothing."

But Aladdin still remained silent. "There is no shame in not knowing what course to take," remarked the sorcerer. Smiling inwardly, he went on. "Allow me to suggest something then. Suppose I open a splendid shop for you and fill it with costly goods, silks and rugs? Soon you will be known as a wealthy merchant." The sorcerer had no intention of doing what he promised, but he would have offered Aladdin the world just now to make the boy trust him.

The crafty villain had judged Aladdin correctly, for the boy was delighted at this suggestion. He loved beautiful things, and the idea of being a respectable merchant with his own fine shop filled him with happiness. So the following day the sorcerer took him to the marketplace. He bought Aladdin handsome clothes and promised him that together they would find the perfect spot to set up a place of business. Aladdin was overjoyed, and he kissed his uncle's hand as they parted. That night the boy could hardly sleep for the plans that filled his head.

Early the following morning, the sorcerer returned. Aladdin's mother blessed him for his kindness and thanked him over and over again.

"I have done nothing I wouldn't do for my own son," replied the sorcerer, pleased with how well his plan was proceeding. "Unfortunately, today the shops are closed, so we can do no business. Instead, I should like to take Aladdin out of the city to see sights he has never seen before. With your permission, we shall not return till evening."

Of course, Aladdin's mother agreed. She stood in the doorway smiling and waving good bye as she watched them disappear down the road. As the two walked arm in arm out of the city, the sorcerer pointed out various sights. They traveled most of the day, and when the sorcerer saw that Aladdin was growing tired, they stopped to rest in a beautiful tree-lined garden. There he loosened the parcel he had brought along with him, and they ate cheese, salted nuts, olives and the sweetest dates. When they had eaten their fill, the sorcerer led them on even farther. Aladdin had never walked so far. He was weary, and as evening approached he asked his uncle if they should consider turning back for home.

"Aladdin, be a man," said the sorcerer with some irritation. "I wish to show you something that is still some distance off."

To keep Aladdin from thinking of home, the sorcerer told him tales of adventure in foreign lands. At last, they reached their destination and the real reason that had brought the sorcerer so far from his home in Morocco. His true purpose was near at hand, and he could hardly conceal his excitement. By now the sky was dark; a full moon shone overhead, giving off an eerie light. The two travelers sat down on the ground to rest.

The fire suddenly exploded, and the earth shook violently beneath their feet.

"This is the place we have been seeking," said the sorcerer. "Quickly, gather some dry sticks and make us a fire."

Aladdin did as he was asked, wondering what possible interest this dry empty spot could hold for anyone. When the fire began to blaze, the sorcerer pulled a small box from his pocket. From the box he took some greenish powder and sprinkled it onto the flames, muttering a mysterious chant in words Aladdin did not understand. The fire suddenly exploded, and the earth shook violently beneath their feet. Aladdin was so frightened that he started to run, but the sorcerer caught him by his collar and struck him so hard across the face that the boy was knocked nearly senseless. Just as abruptly, the fire died down, revealing a black marble slab with a brass chain where a moment earlier there had been nothing but dry ground.

Everything became deathly still. None of the familiar sounds of night could be heard. Not a cricket or even a breeze stirred the uneasy quiet. In the silence, Aladdin turned to face the sorcerer. His face stung from the harsh blow he had received, and he struggled to fight back tears.

"Uncle, what have I done to deserve your anger?"

"Forgive me, my son," said the sorcerer in a gentle tone. "I struck you to make a man of you. You are my beloved nephew, and you must trust me. Remember, I am your uncle, your dead father's brother, and you must do as I tell you. Now, listen carefully. By my great magic, I have uncovered this marble slab that has been hidden under the earth for centuries. Do as I say, and you shall see a wonder beyond compare. You alone may lift this slab to discover a treasure no man can equal. Beneath this stone lies a staircase that will lead you to it. Since only you can enter, I must stay behind and wait. But first take my ring and place it on your finger." The sorcerer took the ring from his own hand and placed it on Aladdin's finger. It was a thick, coarsely made ring of heavy gold, with an uncut green gem the size of a large cherrystone that glittered in the moonlight. Aladdin did not have a chance to see the inscription written in Persian inside. It read "Rise again."

"This ring," the sorcerer cautioned, "will protect you from all harm. Now, you must be brave, and do what your destiny has marked you for. Together we will share the hidden wealth below. Be quick, lift the slab by its chain and you will see that everything I have told you is true."

"But, Uncle, I'm not strong enough to lift it by myself," said Aladdin. "Please, come help me."

The sorcerer refused, saying, "Aladdin, I've told you no one else can raise the stone but *you*. If I help you, all will be lost. Take hold of the chain and try, repeating your name as you do; the stone will obey you, I promise."

Mustering all his strength, Aladdin pulled at the brass chain and pronounced his name. At once, the stone moved away easily, revealing a deep, vaulted chamber. To his surprise, a dozen or more steps led down into a gem-studded cave that glittered in the dim light.

"Aladdin," called the sorcerer. "You must be careful and remember everything I tell you to the last detail. When you reach the bottom of the stairs, you will find four huge rooms. Each will be directly off the main hall, and they are filled with gold and silver. Do not enter any of these rooms. Touch nothing and be certain not even to brush your robe against the walls or doorways. I warn you, you will regret it the rest of your days if you do not heed me. Should you be so careless as to do so, you will be imprisoned within black stone, and I doubt that even I will be able to save you. Instead, follow the hall to the end. There you will find a sunken garden filled with the most spectacular fruit trees. Climb the stone steps that lead up to the garden's terrace and take down the oil lamp that hangs from the great willow tree. Pour out the oil in the lamp, saying your name as you did before. Then hide the lamp under your garments. Should any of the oil drop on you, do not concern yourself, for it is not ordinary oil and will leave no trace. If you wish, you may then stop to pick any of the fruit you see hanging from the trees in the garden. But hurry back to me; I will be waiting impatiently for your return.

"Now, good luck. And be brave, for by this awesome deed you

will no longer be a child but a grown man who will have earned his destiny. My ring will protect you from evil so long as you follow every detail of my instructions. Once you complete this task, you shall be the richest man in the world!"

Aladdin believed all the sorcerer told him. With the success of having lifted the marble stone so effortlessly, his courage had already returned. He smiled bravely at the sorcerer and then, turning, he jumped to the first step and hurried down the staircase.

Everything was just as the sorcerer had described. There to the right and left of the hallway were the four dangerous rooms filled with gold and silver. Cautiously, he passed them, hugging his garments close so that he touched nothing. At last, he found his way to the sunken garden. Breathless, he climbed the steps to the terrace and took hold of the oil lamp. Repeating his name, he poured out the oil and fastened the lamp under his robe. Only then did he take time to marvel at the enchanted world surrounding him. Shimmering light gleamed in all directions from the heavily laden fruit trees. Diamonds, rubies, emeralds and topaz stones hung from every bough. His poverty had taught him nothing of such things, and Aladdin thought they were just lovely glass objects instead of precious jewels, each large enough to command a king's ransom. But they glittered so brightly that he couldn't resist gathering them till his pockets and arms were filled to overflowing.

Encumbered by the costly stones, he turned back through the chamber. He struggled up the staircase, but found he could not manage to climb the final step, which was higher than the rest.

"Uncle, please give me your hand and pull me up," called Aladdin.

"Give me the lamp, my boy. The weight of it is preventing you from lifting yourself," replied the sorcerer anxiously.

But Aladdin was too burdened with his jewels to get at the lamp. "My arms are too full. I cannot. Just give me your hand, and you shall have the lamp as soon as I'm up," answered the boy.

The sorcerer's sole aim was to gain the lamp, and he rashly assumed that the boy had realized its worth and wished to keep it for

At last, he found his way to the sunken garden.

himself. Very angry, he repeated his demand again, but Aladdin was still unable to climb the step. The sorcerer flew into a wild rage. He rushed to the fire, cast more green powder into the flames and shouted another incantation. With a hollow moan, the earth closed over Aladdin, leaving him entombed beneath the ground in utter darkness.

*I*n those final moments, Aladdin finally saw the sorcerer for what he was—not his uncle, but a treacherous stranger. The sorcerer's studies over forty years had brought him to the discovery that a vast treasure lay hidden in the ground far from his homeland of Morocco but just outside the desert city where Aladdin lived. Delving further, he learned the time was right: The stars were in the proper position for the treasure to be uncovered. But this treasure could only belong to the man who possessed the enchanted lamp that hung in the sunken garden. The owner of the lamp would be the most powerful in all the wide world; nothing he wished for could be denied him. Only one boy in the sorcerer's lifetime was destined to gain that lamp. To his chagrin, the stars cast that boy to be none other than *Aladdin*. Centuries before, too long for anyone to reckon, Aladdin's ancestors had ruled the lamp. The sands of time had buried these secrets along with the enchanted lamp, waiting only for Aladdin to come and uncover them.

Even with this knowledge, the sorcerer was determined to have the lamp. So he made the journey from Morocco and deceived Aladdin ruthlessly in order to steal it. But when he thought he might not get it, his rage overwhelmed him, and he shut Aladdin up in the ground. Then, without a backward glance, he hastened away for the long journey back to Morocco.

Meanwhile, Aladdin cried out to be released from his tomb. But the sorcerer was long gone, and not another living soul could hear him. Although he shouted for help, Aladdin knew it was hopeless. He realized the evil sorcerer was not his uncle and would never raise a finger to help him.

Aladdin let the jewels fall from his arms, for they would do him no good now. He heard them tumble down the staircase in the otherwise silent darkness. Despair engulfed him, and he sat down and began to weep. For two long days, he remained a prisoner, too terrified to move for fear of touching some magical object that might imprison him in stone as the sorcerer had warned. The grim reality of his position could have destroyed him, but some hidden resource gave him strength. Just as the sorcerer had predicted, Aladdin's boyishness fell away in the face of his harsh predicament.

On the third morning, he awoke hungry and thirsty. Restlessly, he twisted the sorcerer's ring upon his finger. Suddenly, there was a burst of green smoke, and a small genie appeared before Aladdin.

"Master of the Ring, I am at your command. Whatever you wish, I will hasten to fulfill," said the genie, with a bow.

The sight of such a creature so shocked Aladdin that he could barely speak. But the sorcerer's words concerning the ring came back to him soon enough. Summoning his courage, he said, "Genie of the Ring, use your powers to free me from this place."

"Master, I hear and will obey," replied the genie.

Before Aladdin took another breath, he was aboveground and free once more. The genie had disappeared, and in the light of day, Aladdin scarcely recognized the spot where he stood. Breathing the fresh air, he rubbed his eyes and felt as though he had just awakened from some cruel dream. The marble slab and the entrance to the cavern were gone. Was it possible that he had imagined everything?

He wondered, but then at his feet he spied the cinders left from the magic fire. No, he thought, certainly it had not been a dream. There the sorcerer had pronounced his incantations, and those ashes were the only remaining proof of the death Aladdin had faced and miraculously escaped.

Exhausted, Aladdin forced himself to make the journey home. When he arrived, his mother rushed to welcome him. Too weak to answer her frantic questions, he fell into her arms, and she helped him to his bed. Soon Aladdin was able to tell her the whole story, and the poor woman wept at the thought that she might have lost her son forever. Then he slept, only waking to drink the thin broth his mother offered him.

With rest, Aladdin's strength returned, but he had not eaten solid food in many days, and his hunger was great. "Mother, I'm so hungry. What is there to eat?"

His mother shook her head sadly, saying, "The broth I gave you is all we had, and I've no money to buy food."

"I still have that lamp the magician thought so valuable. Perhaps we can sell it," suggested Aladdin.

She took the lamp from Aladdin and carried it to the kitchen to clean before bringing it to the market. She mixed some lemon juice with sand and began rubbing the tarnish from the lamp's surface. Suddenly, the tiny room filled with blood red smoke, and a monstrous genie towered over her.

"Mistress, the genie of the lamp has heard your summons. Command, and I shall obey."

Her screams brought Aladdin rushing in. When he saw the genie and heard his words, Aladdin snatched up the lamp, saying, "We are hungry. Please, good genie, bring us something to eat."

The genie vanished, and in a moment returned to lay before them a sumptuous meal on twelve plates of the finest silver. Then, bowing to them both, he disappeared. Aladdin sat down immediately and began to eat, but his mother hesitated.

"Aladdin, in days of old, genies did appear to people, but never in my lifetime have I heard that such a thing could still take place. Is this the same creature that saved you from the cavern?"

"No, Mother, this is the genie of the lamp; he told you so himself. The other was the genie of the ring that I still wear upon my finger."

"Aladdin, swear to me that you will get rid of these objects of enchantment. They can do us no good."

"What harm can there be in eating this food? Believe me, it is delicious," said Aladdin. "As for it doing me no good, if it were not for the genie of the ring, I would still be buried under the ground. Now, you are hungry, too; sit down and eat with me."

Aladdin's mother did as he bade her, but she was still troubled. "Aladdin, I cannot bear the sight of such awesome creatures. They frighten me too much. Promise me I will never have to see them again."

"Ever since I was a child I have happily obeyed you," Aladdin told her gently. "You shall not be troubled by these genies, but I cannot give up the ring or the lamp. For as long as we have them, we shall never be poor or hungry again. I think the magician knew the value of the lamp, or he would not have come so very far to get it. Remember, he didn't tell me to bring him silver or gold from the cavern. No, he asked only for the lamp. This enchanted lamp," said Aladdin, holding it up before his mother. "And when I couldn't give it to him, he tried to kill me. Believe me, Mother, we must keep the lamp and tell no one that we have it."

Aladdin's mother looked silently upon her son. She thought, *He has changed; he's not the boy he was. He seems older and wiser than his years—so quickly he has grown into a man.* She smiled fondly at him and nodded her head. "Very well," she told him. "We shall do as you wish."

For two days Aladdin and his mother feasted on the food the genie of the enchanted lamp had brought them. When there was nothing left, Aladdin took the plates one by one and went to the marketplace

"Mistress, the genie of the lamp has heard your summons. Command, and I shall obey."

to sell them. Since he knew nothing of the value of silver, he sold them for a fraction of their true worth to a dishonest merchant. Still, it was more money than the poor young man had ever seen. Aladdin gave his mother the money, and, with it, she was able to buy whatever they needed for some weeks. But when even this money ran out, Aladdin knew he must use the lamp again. He chose a moment when his mother was out of the house; then he rubbed the lamp three times and called forth the powerful genie.

"Master of the Lamp, ask what you wish."

"Good genie, bring me food on plates as before," asked Aladdin.

No sooner had Aladdin finished speaking than the genie was gone and back again. He set before Aladdin twelve silver plates, each filled with steaming hot food. Then, bowing low, the genie vanished. Aladdin's mouth watered at the sight of such delicacies, not knowing which to choose from first. There was thick golden soup, along with spiced meats wrapped in light pastry, roasted lamb with fresh herbs and sweet honey-soaked cakes, all sending a delicious fragrance through the tiny house.

When his mother returned from her errand, Aladdin called to her, "Look, Mother, what a magnificent feast awaits you."

The tempting aroma was irresistible, and she sat down at once to join him, saying, "Even if I can't abide the sight of your genie, how can I refuse his wonderful meal? His feasts are fit for a king," she said, smiling. "I bless him and you, my dear son, and may we never regret it."

What was not finished that night was stored for the following days. When even this was consumed, Aladdin again set out with one of the silver plates to sell. As it happened, the dishonest merchant who had bought the other plates was not in his shop that day. So the young man sought another, where the owner was known for his honesty in business. The merchant examined the silver plate and weighed it carefully.

"Have you sold other plates of this kind?" asked the merchant.

"Yes. I have received the handsome sum of one gold dinar from Abdul the goldsmith," replied Aladdin.

"You have been cheated, then. This silver is the finest I've ever seen and you should command seventy dinars at least. I will pay that much should you wish to sell it."

Aladdin sold the plate to the merchant and the other eleven as well. He began to realize that there was much he did not know. He took to spending time in the marketplace examining the goods and watching the dealers. When he could, Aladdin asked questions, and often the honest merchant who had bought his plates advised him.

With the passage of time, Aladdin taught himself what was quality and what was not, who was honest and who was not. He also learned, to his regret, that in the cavern where he was once prisoner, what he had thought were lovely glass fruits hanging from the trees in the sunken garden were really precious gems. So precious, in fact, that in none of the expensive jewel shops he entered did he ever find gems to equal the size and quality of those that had filled his arms and pockets to overflowing. Over the next two years, he was often to shake his head with a wistful smile upon his lips at the thought of the priceless jewels he left behind. But there was no greed in him, and he never thought to ask the genie of the lamp for more than what he needed for himself and his mother.

Aladdin and his mother were no longer poor. They lived comfortably, if modestly, and time passed agreeably for them both. Aladdin was now about seventeen years old and had grown tall and handsome. Girls smiled at him and tried to gain his affection, but, as yet, romantic love was something he knew nothing about.

Then, one day, as Aladdin was walking through the marketplace, he saw a group of the sultan's heralds riding through the main square on horseback. They shouted out a message from the sultan for all to hear.

"The sultan's daughter, the princess Badoura, today desires to visit the public baths. That she may do so unseen and undisturbed, the sultan has ordered everyone else to remain home. Every door must be closed, and every window shuttered. Under pain of death, no one is to look upon the royal princess. He who disobeys this proclamation will be caught and killed; his death will be on his own head for defying the great sultan's decree."

Even before the heralds finished speaking, Aladdin was seized with a longing to do what had been forbidden. The princess was thought to be the most beautiful young woman in the world, and though it might mean death to Aladdin, he determined to risk it for the chance to gaze upon her.

Aladdin hurried to the public baths and hid himself behind a door in the entranceway. When the streets were cleared, the shops shut up and the houses closed tight, the princess Badoura arrived at the baths with her companions. As she entered, she let her veil fall, and Aladdin saw her face for the first time.

You have no doubt heard of the singing of mermaids that lures sailors to destruction. The sailor at the helm leaves the tiller and leans over the prow to listen with the others. Unguided, the ship steers no more, but drives before the wind heedless of wreck or drowning. Aladdin's expression was like that of such a mariner; on his lips was the pale smile of one who hears sweet music far off or sees a vision all his own.

"Truly," he murmured to himself, "she is more beautiful than anyone supposed."

He felt dazed and confused by new emotions he did not under stand, and long after she had passed him, these unfamiliar sensations lingered. His face flushed, and he felt a surge of joy and sadness all at the same moment. At no time had he ever felt anything like this. He realized that in that single instant, he had fallen in love with the princess. It was as though, without even being aware, he had been searching the whole of his existence for her. His happiness was in the knowledge that he had finally found her, and his sadness sprang from the conviction that he would never love another.

When Aladdin was certain that it was safe, he left his hiding place and returned home. But he could not get the sight of the princess out of his mind. He would not eat and could not sleep. His mother marked the startling change in her son and asked him the reason.

"I have seen the face of the princess Badoura," said Aladdin. "She shines like the brightest star in the heavens. She is a rare jewel among the gray stones of life. I fear I cannot live without her. I must make her my wife."

His mother was shocked. "Live without her! Son, you will not live

He realized that in that single instant, he had fallen in love with the princess.

another day should the sultan hear of this. Put this idea from your mind. It is madness."

"I cannot," Aladdin told her. "I have tried to forget her. I would rather die than live without at least trying to win her love. I have a plan—only you must help me."

Seeing Aladdin in such anguish moved his mother to listen. She embraced him and said, "Very well, tell me what it is you need me to do, and I shall try."

"Here is my plan. The sultan is a just king, and on certain days he hears the petitions of his subjects. No one who presents a request or grievance to him on such a day goes away without feeling he has been heard and dealt with fairly. Is this not true?"

His mother nodded in agreement. "Yes, yes. He is a just king. I do not deny that he is. But even so, what does this have to do with your plan?"

"I am coming to that," continued Aladdin. "I ask you to go to the sultan and present my petition. Tell him I solemnly love his daughter and wish for her hand in marriage."

The woman was thunderstruck. "Have you gone completely mad?" she cried. "Your father was the poorest tailor in this city. We are of the humblest stock! The sultan will strike me dead for making such an outrageous request. Think what you're saying, Aladdin. Your love for the royal princess has made you crazy. The sultan intends to give his daughter—mind you, his only child—to some high-ranking prince, not to a commoner! Besides, those who come before the sultan, even in small matters, bring with them some gift to honor him. What could you possibly give his majesty that would justify such an insane proposal?"

"I have thought of this already. Don't forget I have a lamp that has so far served us well."

His mother shook her head. "Food the lamp has given you. Silver plates. What use does the sultan have for these things? No, Aladdin.

I must see that I get you to a doctor, for this madness has overcome you."

"I do not need a doctor, Mother. Leave it to me to think of something that will warm the sultan to my request."

The two of them talked through the night, and at dawn Aladdin's mother, still not convinced, finally went to sleep. Then Aladdin took the lamp from its hiding place and, rubbing it three times, he brought forth the genie.

"Bring me a plate filled with the jewels that hang from the trees in the sunken garden where I found the lamp."

"I hear, Master. And I will obey," answered the genie. But he paused for a moment, and a wise, almost imperceptible smile crossed his lips. Then, nodding, as if to say, "At last, Aladdin, you begin to recognize the great powers of the lamp," he vanished.

Almost immediately the genie returned, carrying at least fifty jewels upon a golden plate. Each bright stone was larger than a man's fist. Aladdin admired their exquisite color and sparkle in the early morning light. He suspected that the value of just one would be quite enough to allow a man to live in luxury for the rest of his life. But he hoped these fifty glittering gems, lying one upon the other in a glorious pyramid, might buy him favor with the father of the woman he loved.

When his mother woke, Aladdin showed her his gift for the sultan. She was breathless from the sight of such beauty, yet she was still worried. "Oh yes, this is a spectacular gift to set before a king, I grant you that. But what on earth shall I say when the sultan asks me who you are? Then he will have my head cut off, I promise you."

"Don't worry yourself with thoughts like this. When the sultan sees my gift, he will not ask. No one able to offer so grand a gift would be asked such a question. Your petition will be well received. The sultan will be so pleased that he will think a great king has asked for his daughter. Now let us wrap the jewels carefully, and you shall take them to the sultan this morning."

The astonishing beauty of the jewels gave the woman courage, and with some further convincing, she agreed to go before the sultan. They wrapped the jewels and the plate in a fine linen cloth, and she was soon on her way. But once she entered the sultan's receiving hall, her newfound courage evaporated. She took a seat in the back of the room and felt too paralyzed to go forward. The entire day she sat in the same spot, too frightened to move, and listened to the other petitioners. As the last person completed his mission, she rose from her chair and slipped out.

When Aladdin saw her return with the parcel, his heart sank, but he said nothing. The next day, his mother set out again. When she arrived, the hall was not yet crowded. She watched the sultan's grand vizier proceed into the court with other noblemen. Soon the hall was filled with courtiers, people of business and common folk set upon some vital errand. At last, the sultan entered. The others stood up in respectful silence as he took his seat upon the throne. Then every-one sat once more, and with a wave of his majesty's hand, the peti-tioners began to be heard one by one in accordance with their rank.

Each petition taken before the sultan was judged with fairness, but many were not heard that day for lack of time. Though Aladdin's mother was one of the first to have arrived, she had not been spoken to, and no one of the court's company had offered to escort her to the throne. When the sultan had retired for the day, and the rest had filed out, she made her way home again.

Aladdin watched her with expectant eyes as she came into the house. She sat down beside him and smiled at him sadly. "Be patient, this is no easy thing you ask of me. The first day, though I left here boldly enough, my courage failed me completely. Today I might have done better, but I didn't have the chance. I will go again tomorrow."

The next morning she returned to the palace hall and was obliged to wait again, but without success. She took herself there each day the hall was open and waited helplessly for an audience with the sultan. At the close of a final session, the sultan himself, who could not help but notice her after so many days, asked her to come forward.

Trembling, Aladdin's mother came toward the mighty sultan; her legs felt weak with the effort and her tongue seemed glued to the roof of her mouth. She fell on her knees before him.

"Good woman, I have seen you come to my hall day after day. Tell me what you wish to ask, so that I may grant it."

Aladdin's mother blessed the sultan and kissed the ground before his feet. "Majesty, I beg you, my plea may sound strange to you. Please hear me without offense."

The sultan was a generous man, and so far his day had gone well enough, leaving him in an indulgent mood. "Whatever you might ask will not go against you. Have no fear of me, dear lady. Speak."

"Great Sultan, I also beg your mercy."

"You have it, now speak at last."

"I also beg that you will not cut off my head for what I must ask."

"I assure you, madam, I am not in the habit of cutting women's heads off. Speak, I command it," said the sultan, with a bemused expression upon his face.

"I have one child, Your Majesty. Aladdin is his name. He is a good son, and I also pray you will not cut off his head," said the woman nervously.

"Praise Allah! I will not cut off his head either," answered the sultan. "Pray continue."

"Thank you, Great Sultan. Then I will go on," said Aladdin's mother with a heavy sigh. "He saw your daughter, the royal princess Badoura, and in that instant fell in love with her. He wishes for her hand in marriage, and though I have begged him to reconsider, he has told me he will die without her. Forgive me and my son for such audacity. A mother can do nothing but try to aid her child in any way she can." Then Aladdin's mother held her breath in terror, awaiting what the sultan would do to her.

The sultan stared down at her impassively. Everyone waited to see what he would do. His face revealed nothing, and his eyes were like marble as he continued to gaze at the terrified woman. Suddenly, he began to laugh, a rich hearty laugh that caused the others in the hall to join him. At last, he stopped and asked, "Now, what do you carry in your bundle?"

Seeing that the sultan was not angry at her, she breathed in relief, and, plucking up her courage, she undid the parcel. The entire hall lit up as the cloth was pulled away from the jewels. It was as though colored flames had been set alight. Those who saw gasped in wonder, and the sultan himself was dazzled.

"Never have I seen such jewels! My own treasury of stones cannot compare to these." Turning to his vizier, he asked, "Don't you agree? Have you ever in your life seen anything so beautiful?"

"Your Majesty is quite correct," replied the astonished grand vizier. "Even in the royal treasury there is nothing of such spectacular quality."

"My son, Aladdin, sends them to you, Majesty," said the good woman bravely.

"I cannot but be much disposed to your son, madam, if I accept his fabulous gift." The sultan turned to his grand vizier once again. "Don't you think the young man who sends me this prize is worthy of the princess? Worthier, my dear vizier, than any other man?"

The vizier was noticeably disturbed, for the sultan had already promised his daughter to the vizier's son.

The vizier whispered into the sultan's ear. "Great Monarch, I beg you to remember that the princess Badoura is already promised to another. Take this gift, for Your Great Highness is certainly entitled to it. But, please, ask for a delay of three months, to see if my son can find a dowry gift greater than this."

The sultan knew that neither the vizier's son nor the richest monarch in the world could find a marriage offering equal to the present Aladdin had given. But he did not wish to offend his chief minister, and so he willingly granted a delay.

"Go to your son," he told the woman. "Tell him my daughter shall be his."

"Go to your son," he told the woman. "Tell him my daughter shall be his. But the wedding must wait three months, as there are, of course, preparations to be made."

Aladdin's mother thanked the sultan and rushed from the hall. Her joy was so great that she could not wait to reach her son.

"Aladdin, Aladdin, you were right! The sultan has granted you his daughter in marriage," she told him as he greeted her.

"Tell me everything, Mother. Leave nothing out to the last detail."

His mother told him what had happened to her from the moment the sultan called her to him. "But one thing troubles me; the sultan's grand vizier at one point whispered to his majesty. I could not hear what was said, but after this the sultan agreed to my request with one stipulation: that you must wait three months before the marriage can take place. I fear the vizier is a cunning man, and he will use his wiles to dissuade the sultan from favoring you."

Although the delay seemed like forever to the young man, he was overjoyed at the news. He embraced his mother and kissed her affectionately. "Mother, I feel I have been dead, and you have given me new life. How can I ever thank you? Now I am not only the richest man in the world, thanks to the enchanted lamp, but also the happiest, thanks to you."

For two months, Aladdin waited patiently. He counted the days and made plans for the future. But then one day, when his mother went off to the marketplace to do her shopping, she was surprised to see that all the shops were closed for a holiday, and the streets were decked with ornaments for a royal celebration. She stopped a passerby and asked him if he knew the reason for the festivities.

"Why, haven't you heard?" the man replied. "The sultan's daughter is to be married to the grand vizier's son this very evening."

"We have been betrayed by the sultan and his minister," Aladdin's mother told him when she arrived home. "The princess Badoura will marry none other than the vizier's son tonight!"

The news filled Aladdin with rage. He felt helpless to do anything to stop the wedding and then, all at once, he remembered the lamp. He took a deep breath, and turning to his mother, he said in a grim voice, "You can be assured that the vizier's son will not enjoy his wedding night."

Aladdin's mother tried to make him explain his meaning, but he said not another word. When night came, he went to his room and locked the door behind him. Then he took out the lamp and rubbed it three times so that the genie appeared.

". . . bring me the vizier's son at the very instant before he enters the bridal chamber for the night."

"Master of the Lamp, I am at your service. Command and I will obey."

"Then listen carefully. The sultan has promised his daughter to me, but tonight he marries her to another. If you are truly the mighty genie I suppose, bring me the vizier's son at the very instant before he enters the bridal chamber for the night."

The genie vanished, and at midnight appeared again with the princess's bridegroom tucked under one of his great arms like a sack of grain. The groom had been carried away so quickly from the door of his new bedroom that Badoura had not even heard his approach. No sooner did the genie set him down on his feet than the young man fell to his knees, weeping in terror.

Aladdin then gave another order, "Good genie, take up this sniveling coward and lock him in the cellar overnight."

"Will there be anything else, Master?" inquired the genie.

"Yes, there is one more thing. But come back to me when you are finished with him, and I shall tell you."

The genie picked up his charge and was off in a flash. When he returned, Aladdin said, "Now I wish you to transport me to the princess's bedchamber. At daybreak, come back to bring me home. Take the vizier's son with you, so you may then leave him in my place."

With the wave of the genie's hand, an ornate carpet appeared, floating in the air. He hoisted Aladdin upon it and then climbed on as well. With another wave of his hand, the magic carpet glided out the window, carrying Aladdin and the genie into the starry night.

In the meantime, the new bride paced her bedroom, wondering what could be keeping her husband. She heard the servants' steps outside her bedroom door as they left to go to bed themselves. Then all grew silent, and she felt a dismal sense of sadness now after the gaiety of the day-long festivities. To dispel it, she lighted the pair of wax candles beside her bed. The oil lamps burned high as well, and the room was bathed in light. It was a beautiful room, even for a princess. The gleaming mosaic floor was covered with splendidly designed carpets, and large silk pillows lay about the room. The great four-post bed was black mahogany, fantastically carved and decorated with gold. At the very top, the carvings joined to form a gigantic royal crown. Thick satin curtains hung down from the top and enclosed the bed.

Badoura felt a chill though the night was warm, and she would have been glad to hear the gossiping voices of the servants in the distance or the footsteps of her new husband. But there was only silence, which somehow made her feel solitary and forlorn.

Finally, snuffing out the lamps and candles, she turned to go to bed. Just then, she heard movement in the room. Thinking it was her husband, she called to him in the darkness. There was no answer. Instead, a lamp was lighted, and Aladdin stood before her.

"Princess, I beg you to hear me out before you sound the alarm. I swear I wish you no harm," he told her gently.

At first, Badoura was too shocked to speak or cry out, but she quickly regained her composure and sat down. She knew no real harm could come to her in her own palace with guards on every floor. This young man might be dangerous, but he was quite handsome and had obviously gone to great lengths to slip into the palace and gain access to her rooms.

Seeing that she was willing to listen, Aladdin began at once to explain. He told her everything that had passed between the sultan and his mother. In conclusion, he added, "You have been promised to me. I have loved you since the moment I saw you. With all my heart, I wish you to be my wife. Because the vizier's son has no right to you, I have seen to it that he shall not be with you this evening. I ask that you allow me to remain here tonight. I will not dishonor you in any way. But I also will not have another take the place that is rightfully mine as your promised husband."

The princess was silent for a few moments while she considered everything Aladdin had told her. She didn't for an instant doubt what he had said. Her instincts told her he was sincere, and she trusted him. In truth, she had no particular love for the vizier's son. In those

"Princess, I beg you to hear me out before you sound the alarm. I swear I wish you no harm," he told her gently.

days, royal weddings were arranged, and no one had thought to ask her opinion in the matter. Inwardly she was amused to hear that Aladdin had disposed of the vizier's son for the evening. She also thought it was very wrong of her father to have given his word in such an important matter and then to have broken it. Certainly, since he had agreed to the match, Aladdin must be a worthy suitor. And now, after seeing and listening to him, she knew that had she been given the choice of either man, she would gladly have picked Aladdin over the other.

"What then do you propose to do this evening?" she asked.

"If you will agree, I shall sleep on this couch till morning and then I will leave. You can trust that I will not trouble you beyond this single request."

"Very well, then," said the princess. "I wish you good luck in your suit and good night." Then she got up and went back to her bed, drawing the heavy curtains behind her.

The next day, good as his word, Aladdin was gone when she awoke. Badoura felt somewhat disappointed that she did not get a chance to see him even briefly before he left. But very shortly after, her father entered the chamber to wish his daughter good morning. She seemed strangely silent, and when she was unwilling to give a reason, he turned to go. It was only then that together they both spied the vizier's son, sitting dejectedly in a shadowy corner. The sultan demanded an explanation, and when neither of the two young people could deliver one, he stormed from the room in a fury.

The sultan found his wife in her own rooms and insisted that she speak to her daughter at once. The princess was willing to tell her mother everything. The queen heard her daughter out, but she could hardly believe what she had been told.

"You were wise not to tell your father this tale. He would surely think you mad. Perhaps it was but a bad dream that only seems real to you this morning. Say nothing to anyone about it, and by this afternoon you will have forgotten it," her mother advised her.

"But, Mother, I am not mad. What I've told you happened truly," Badoura insisted.

Although her mother still doubted the story, she decided to humor her daughter. "Very well, my dear. Nevertheless, I still wish you to keep silent about it and allow me to speak to your father."

Returning to her husband, the queen told him that their daughter had had a bad dream, but she was feeling much better.

The wedding festivities continued that day and well into the evening. But that night, the events of the previous one were repeated. The bridegroom was whisked away, and Aladdin appeared in his place. He and the princess passed as comfortable a night as possible; Aladdin kept to his couch and did not disturb her, but Badoura found she was becoming quite fond of her new companion.

The next morning when the sultan awoke, his first thoughts were of his daughter. He dressed hastily and went directly to her rooms to see if she had passed a peaceful night. Although everything seemed in order, Badoura again evaded his questions.

Unused to being defied, the sultan grew angry. "I demand to know the reason for your odd behavior."

Badoura only replied, "You, Father, know the true cause better than I. The honorable thing would be for you to dissolve the marriage."

Her last statement totally mystified the sultan. He had put the appearance of Aladdin's mother completely out of his mind, and his daughter's words failed to remind him of it. Getting nowhere with her, the sultan took her husband aside.

"I will have your head, if you have mistreated the princess. Tell me at once, what has passed between you? This morning she demanded that your marriage be dissolved."

"Majesty, I have not even seen her for two nights. Instead, I have spent the last two evenings in the most embarrassing discomfort. Though I love your daughter, I, too, wish to be released from my marriage vows."

"Very well," said the exasperated sultan. "I pronounce the marriage null and void."

The celebrations ceased abruptly. The vizier's son was seen leaving the palace with his head bowed in disgrace. The common people of the city wondered at the reason, but Aladdin, knowing the cause, rejoiced.

The three-month waiting period soon was over, and Aladdin sent his mother back to the palace. Though the sultan had forgotten his promise, when he saw the old woman enter the receiving hall, he suddenly remembered.

Turning away, he said to his minister, "Vizier, there is that woman again. You do remember her, don't you? She is the one who brought me those incredible jewels. Look at her; it's obvious that she is of the humblest lineage. How can I give the princess to her son?"

The grand vizier was still bitter and resentful over his son's humiliating rejection. He burned with jealousy to think that anyone else would have the honor his son had forfeited. "Majesty, tell her that her son must deliver you a dowry gift of such proportion that it will be impossible for him to accomplish it. Then you will be rid of them at last," advised the vizier.

"That is it, of course," said the sultan. "Something no one could ever give us."

He called the woman to him. After she made her bows and wished him well, he said to her, "Madam, tell your son that before he can have my consent for the marriage to my daughter, he must present us with a dowry gift befitting her. Therefore, I expect forty gold plates filled with jewels of the quality you presented at your last visit. They should be carried to me by forty slaves and escorted by forty more. Only then can the wedding take place as promised."

The woman left the sultan crestfallen. How in the world could her son accomplish this outlandish task? Her news was met by Aladdin's laughter. "Very well, I will not disappoint our king. He shall have his gold plates and more jewels tomorrow," he told her.

Aladdin awoke just before dawn. He took up the lamp and rubbed it three times. All at once, the magnificent genie of the lamp appeared.

"Master, what is your wish?"

"The sultan has agreed to allow me to wed his daughter on one condition. I must have forty plates of purest gold filled with jewels from the enchanted garden. These plates must be carried by forty slaves attended by forty more. It will please me if you bring them without delay."

"It shall be done, Master," answered the genie.

Instantly, the genie disappeared and, after a few moments, returned with forty lovely young women, each escorted by a young man. The young women carried dishes of gold filled with glorious gems. The genie bowed before Aladdin and asked if there was anything else he might wish.

"Thank you, good genie," said Aladdin. "I shall require nothing more for the moment."

Shortly after the genie had vanished, Aladdin's mother awoke and was very much astonished to see her tiny home crowded with so many people.

"Aladdin, is this the work of your lamp?" she managed to ask.

"Yes, indeed," he told her. "Now, there is not a moment to lose. Lead the way, mother, for I wish you to take my dowry gift to the sultan immediately. When he sees this, he will know I am not a man to be trifled with, regardless of what his grand vizier may say to the contrary."

Aladdin opened the door of the house, sending the young men and women out in pairs to follow his mother. The assembly filled the streets, and those who saw them stopped and stared at the amazing spectacle. The forty young women were draped in exquisitely colored robes woven with gold thread, their hems and sleeves studded with precious jewels. The plates they held high above their lovely heads and the fiery light from the jewels shone brightly, hurting the eyes of those who watched.

*A*ll along the way passersby stopped and stared in disbelief as Aladdin's mother and her company proceeded toward the palace.

Like a glittering serpent, the procession wound its way through the city. At length they came into the palace courtyard. The guards and their commanders stood frozen in amazement at the beauty of the women and the wealth they brought with them.

A courtier tore himself away from the sight and hurried to the sultan to tell him of the wondrous arrival. With her head held high, Aladdin's mother led the group before the king. They bowed as one body, and when the sultan acknowledged their greeting, each girl laid her gift at his feet.

At the sight of all this splendor, the sultan was speechless. He saw the beauty of the company and the brilliance of the jewels, but could not believe it. At last, he came to himself and congratulated Aladdin's mother, sending salutations to her most remarkable son. Then he ordered that the bridal gifts be sent to Badoura.

When the group was led out of the hall with the jewels, Aladdin's mother said, "These gifts and more my son wishes to bestow upon your daughter. Give your consent to their wedding, and the princess will have a husband who will grant her every desire gladly. Surely, Your Highness, you will not deny his proposal now."

Before the sultan had a chance to speak, the vizier, who had been even more astonished than the sultan by Aladdin's spectacular gift, came close to the king and began to whisper in his ear. He was still eaten up with envy, and realizing that now the sultan seemed much disposed to grant Aladdin the princess, he was frantic to prevent it.

"Your Majesty, nothing this upstart has given makes him worthy of the princess! I beg you to deny him his request for her hand."

But this time the sultan was not to be persuaded by the vizier's words. "Vizier, if this young man does not deserve my daughter, then there is not one living who does." Turning back to Aladdin's mother, he said, "Good woman, I am much pleased with your son. Tell him I accept his dowry gifts. My daughter shall be his bride. Bring him to the palace, so I may have the honor of meeting my new son-in-law. The wedding contract shall be signed this very evening."

Swiftly the woman left the palace and hurried home to her son. By the look on her face when she came through the door, Aladdin knew success was at hand. He kissed his mother gratefully and embraced her.

"Now, we must prepare ourselves to meet the king," he told her.

He sent his mother off to ready herself and retired to his room. Taking up the lamp, Aladdin summoned the genie.

At once the genie of the lamp appeared. "Master, I am here. What is your wish?"

"Good genie, you have served me well. The sultan has finally consented to the marriage. I am to meet with him today, and the wedding contract will be signed this very evening. Please bring me what is necessary so that I may present myself with all the pomp and circumstance expected of a great king."

With the wave of the genie's hand, a group of servants appeared to minister to Aladdin's needs. They bathed him with scented soap and rose water. They trimmed his hair and shaved him. The finest garments were then presented to him, and he was helped to dress. Other servants were sent to his mother. Clothes and jewels befitting a queen were given to her to wear. When Aladdin was dressed, he stood before the mirror admiring himself. Instead of the poor tailor's son he had been, he now had the appearance and manner of a great king. Then the genie waved his hand again, and the servants disappeared.

At that moment a golden carriage drawn by twelve pure white Arabian horses rolled up and stopped at the door of the house. Twelve magnificently dressed young women climbed out to escort Aladdin's mother to the palace. Two dozen horsemen in royal blue livery stood waiting to accompany Aladdin. The genie led Aladdin to a black Arabian stallion and handed him the animal's jeweled bridle. Aladdin mounted his horse as still more servants appeared on foot, wearing richly colored garments. In their arms they carried great pots of gold coins. Aladdin instructed them to toss the coins to the crowds that stood by, watching in awe as the regal company set out for the palace.

The crowds praised Aladdin for his generosity, and, though they knew him to be the son of a poor tailor, no one envied him or wished him anything but happiness.

Meanwhile, the sultan was busy making ready for his new son-in-law's arrival. First, he hurried to his daughter to tell her of his decision. When he entered her room, he dismissed all the servants so they could be alone. Then he sat Badoura down and told her all that had taken place.

"Do you not think these dowry gifts make this young man a worthy husband for you?" he asked her.

"I am well pleased, Father. Aladdin is the man I would choose for my husband," she said, smiling. "Do not fear for my happiness. You have made the right decision concerning me."

Delighted, the sultan left her to prepare for the festivities. He gathered his dignitaries around him and stationed nobles at the entrance of the palace to welcome Aladdin. A long carpet was rolled out, and when all was in readiness, Aladdin and his entourage arrived.

Noblemen hastened to greet Aladdin as he dismounted from his horse, and they led him and his mother to the king. When Aladdin stood before the king, he attempted to kneel in respect, as was the

Aladdin mounted his horse as still more servants appeared on
foot, wearing richly colored garments.

custom. But the sultan rose from his throne and stepped forward to prevent it. Instead, he embraced the young man and made him sit at the right of the throne.

When they had exchanged greetings, Aladdin told the sultan, "Sire, you have been gracious indeed to grant that your daughter may marry me though I'm not of royal blood and my father was one of the poorest tailors in your city. I am unworthy of the great honor you pay me. I only wish I had words to thank you sufficiently. The fates have been kind to me and have given me great fortune. May I always deserve it and make myself worthy of the honor you have given me today. I would like to ask that you grant me a piece of land where, with your permission, I will build a palace grand enough for the princess Badoura."

As the king listened to Aladdin's words and looked upon his mother dressed in all her finery, he marveled at them both. This young man appeared as cultured and well mannered as a king. He made no pretense of his origin. What was more, the modesty with which Aladdin spoke impressed the great monarch.

"My son, I only wish that destiny had brought us together sooner," said the sultan with sincerity.

The musicians were ordered to begin playing, and the wedding festivities began. In the royal dining hall, the sultan sat at the head of the long table and bade Aladdin sit at his right in the place of honor. The other nobles, ministers and dignitaries took their seats, each according to their rank. Throughout the evening, the sultan and Aladdin talked and joked together. Aladdin spoke with wisdom and wit, as though he were of the noblest birth. The others, as well as the sultan, noticed this and marked it; by the end of the evening, there was no one who was not impressed by the young man. Everyone enjoyed the evening except the grand vizier, who was more consumed by jealousy than ever.

At the close of the entertainment, the wedding contract was signed and witnessed. When this had been completed, Aladdin rose to make his farewells, but the sultan stopped him.

"Why are you leaving, my son? The contract is only just signed, and the celebration will continue. Tell me, what troubles you?"

"Your Royal Majesty," said Aladdin, "I wish to build Badoura a magnificent palace. I cannot rest till this is finished, for only then can I be the husband she deserves."

"If this is the case, take whatever land in my domain you wish for that purpose. However, it would please me greatly if you would choose to set it on the great square before my own palace."

"I would never have presumed to ask to be so honored, Your Majesty," replied Aladdin. "But since you have suggested it, I gladly accept."

Aladdin then took his leave, and when he arrived home, he brought out the enchanted lamp and rubbed it three times. In a cloud of red smoke, the genie appeared.

"Ask what you will, Master," said the genie. "I am here to serve you."

Aladdin told him what was needed and asked that the genie dispatch his request with the least possible delay. "Please, good genie, let my palace be wonderful to the eye and filled with the comforts that any queen would desire."

Together they discussed the details of the palace. Aladdin asked that there might me a dome in the center with twenty-four windows framed in gold and inlaid with rare jewels. "But I would like you to leave the last window unfinished for a special purpose of my own. On the day that the palace is built, I will wed the princess. So that all the common people will share my joy, see to it that servants pass among the crowds giving gifts of gold to everyone."

"It shall be done as you wish, Master," said the genie, and then he vanished.

At daybreak, Aladdin was awakened by the genie. They climbed upon the magic carpet, and in an instant they arrived at the entrance to Aladdin's new palace. It was truly more wonderful and more beautiful than the young man could have hoped. The outer walls were glowing white marble decorated with lapis and striking mosaics.

On entering, the genie first took him to the treasury, where gold and silver overflowed from every coffer. In the kitchen, the cooks were preparing the morning feast. Their pots were made of gold, and every delicacy was on hand. The dining hall walls were covered with costly tapestries, and a long banquet table gleamed in the sunlight that spilled through tall arched windows. The table settings were made of purest gold, and a diamond chandelier hung from the great vaulted ceiling.

From here, Aladdin was taken to his own chamber, where servants awaited him and rich garments of heavy embroidered silk filled his closets. Room after room housed marvels and treasures beyond description. The princess's chamber would have been the envy of a goddess. The bed was made of darkest mahogany inlaid with emeralds, rubies, diamonds and opals. The carpets were of thick woven silk, and their brilliant designs dazzled the eye. Her windows looked out on her own private garden. The most beautiful jewels of nature were there for her pleasure. Exotic animals and birds, gentle and affectionate, played with her ladies-in-waiting. Trees from all parts of the world grew in lush splendor and rare flowers bloomed in abundance. Orchids and roses, lilies and cherry blossoms gracefully bent their boughs low in radiant profusion.

Finally, Aladdin was ushered to the stables, where the finest Arabian horses, standing in their stalls, tossed their handsome heads at his arrival.

In the center of the palace, there stood a dome of unsurpassable beauty, set with twenty-four windows. Twenty-three were encrusted with precious stones that sparkled in the early morning sun. Just as Aladdin had requested, the twenty-fourth window was left bare. He hoped that the sultan would have it completed as his wedding gift to the couple.

Aladdin turned to the genie, who stood at his side. "Everything is more splendid than I could have dreamed possible. You have made me overjoyed, and I thank you."

*T*hat morning, when the sultan awakened, he looked out his window and fell back in disbelief. He rubbed his sleepy eyes and shook his head, then he looked out the window again. But what he had first seen was still there in all its grandeur: The palace for Badoura had been built in one night by his son-in-law.

At that moment, the vizier entered the sultan's chamber. He, too, was astounded at the sight he was called upon to witness.

"Your Majesty," said the suspicious vizier, "beware of this Aladdin; no king, not even the richest man in the world, could have built this edifice in one night. This is the work of magic, and I fear for your daughter."

The sultan grew angry at these words. "You surprise me, my friend. Is there nothing good you can say about this young man? It is obvious you are jealous of him, and it begins to distort your powers of reasoning. The man who presented me with those priceless jewels for a dowry gift surely could have built this palace in one night."

Not wishing to bring further disfavor upon himself, the vizier kept silent. If the sultan could speak so forcefully on Aladdin's behalf, all the vizier could do was wait and see.

In the meantime, Aladdin gave orders to his servants to go into the streets of the city and, in celebration of his good fortune, distribute gold to the people. When this was done, the people of the city praised Aladdin and loved him for his generosity.

At the sultan's palace, Aladdin was greeted by his father-in-law. They embraced warmly and the wedding banquet commenced. Poor and rich alike were welcomed into the palace on this great day, and all rejoiced.

When the banquet came to a close, Aladdin took the hand of Badoura and led her out of the hall. Everyone filed out to watch the bride and bridegroom as they departed. A long carpet, ordered by Aladdin, ran the length of the path reaching from the sultan's palace to his own so that his beloved princess could walk to her new home in the greatest comfort.

Aladdin's mother joined the couple and together they toured the new palace. The princess was overwhelmed by all she saw. Finally they came to her own rooms, and Badoura praised Aladdin for every detail he had designed for her. Then Aladdin lifted her veil and kissed her tenderly. She was, he thought, even more lovely than he remembered her.

"All this and more I would do for you, my beloved wife."

The princess pressed his hand and smiled lovingly at her husband. Whispering to him so that no one else could hear, she said, "Aladdin, today I am happier than I ever dreamed I could be. I've prayed that we would one day be together like this; I have loved you since we first met."

They sat at a low table, and servants brought the couple wine and sweetmeats. While they dined, musical instruments were taken up by their servants and soft melodies played. Badoura listened with pleasure as she held Aladdin's hand in hers, and her eyes glowed with happiness. That night, it seemed to the two of them that nothing could mar their love.

Next day, Aladdin invited the sultan to visit them and view the palace. As soon as the sultan arrived, he embraced Aladdin as though he were his own son. He clasped his daughter in his arms and kissed her forehead. As he gazed into her bright eyes, he knew without question that she loved her new husband with all her heart.

The sultan complimented Aladdin on all he saw, but something puzzled him as he stood under the glittering dome of jewels. He had caught sight of the unfinished window and wondered at it.

"Poor window, why, I wonder, have you been left incomplete in the face of all this glorious extravagance?" Turning to Aladdin, he asked, "My son, were you so rushed to build your magnificent palace that you did not have time to finish this last window?"

Though this was not true, Aladdin hastened to agree. Then the sultan said, "Allow me to finish it. The completion of this window shall be my wedding gift to you and Badoura."

At once the king sent word to his jewelers and goldsmiths to take what was needed from his own treasuries in order to create a window equal to the others.

Every day the sultan went to the palace to inspect the results of his workmen's progress. But each day he was dismayed to find that it was still not finished. What was more, that which had been done was not nearly as skillfully crafted as the other twenty-three windows. When the jewelers exhausted the supply of jewels in the sultan's treasury, they were sent far and wide to purchase more. Still there were not enough, and the sultan grew impatient.

"Your Royal Highness," said the chief craftsman, "though we have searched, it is impossible to find jewels of similar size and quality to complete the task you have set for us."

That night Aladdin rubbed his lamp, and the genie appeared to him. "Master, how can I serve you?"

"Please return the sultan's jewels to his treasury. And now it would please me if you would finish the last window in the palace's central dome."

"It shall be done immediately, Master," replied the genie with a bow.

The following morning when the craftsmen arrived to begin their labor, they were shocked to find the window quite complete to the last glittering jewel. They hurried to the sultan to tell him, but found

The sultan complimented Aladdin on all he saw, but something puzzled him as he stood under the glittering dome of jewels.

his majesty with the treasurer, who was at the very point of inform-
ing him that all his jewels had been returned.

"Has Aladdin sent no message to explain?" asked the sultan.

No, was their reply. So the sultan went himself to seek the answer.
He found Aladdin standing beneath the completed dome. "Why did
you finish this, my son?" asked the sultan.

"Majesty, too late I realized that your generous offer was more
than I deserved. The gift of your daughter is certainly more than
enough. She is the greatest jewel in the world. What is more, the very
land on which my palace stands was granted to us by you."

"Aladdin! You are a worthy man in every way. You have even
been able to finish this window when all my jewelers and craftsmen
have failed. Never do you cease to amaze me." With that, the sultan
laughed good-naturedly and shook his head at his own folly for ever
doubting this remarkable man.

Day after day Aladdin and Badoura went out to the people of the
city, distributing gold to the sick, the poor and the hungry. Their
kindness spread throughout the domain, and all who talked of them
spoke with loving praise. The couple entertained elegantly; their
visitors from far and near could not help but be moved by the affection the two had for one another.

The sultan appointed Aladdin chief commander of his armies. In
time of war, when armies rode against the kingdom, Aladdin's courage and skillful tactics won him battle after bloody battle till the
opposing forces were defeated and peace was restored. After his
victories, he was welcomed back to the city in triumph. The people
cheered him in the streets as he rode past, and the sultan waited outside his palace beside Badoura and Aladdin's mother to greet him. At
the sight of her husband, Badoura rushed to embrace him, weeping
with relief to have Aladdin safely home with her again.

Great was their happiness that day and for many days following.
Each soldier and citizen of the kingdom looked to Aladdin as their
hero, for his modesty and valor distinguished him above all others.

Meanwhile, in far-off Morocco, the wicked sorcerer worked in his tower hidden high on a secluded hill. He had not forgotten the enchanted lamp, and he still longed to possess it. One day he spread his divining sands, carefully making calculations to pinpoint the lamp's exact whereabouts. But the lamp was not where he expected it to be. He spread the sands a second time and was further confused. Anxiously, he turned to his crystal ball, searching for proof that Aladdin had truly perished after he had sealed him in the cavern of treasures.

By the sorcerer's magic art, he saw that the boy he had left to die certainly had not done so. Instead, the poor tailor's son had escaped to grow and prosper. He had married a fair princess and now lived in honor and the greatest of wealth.

The sorcerer did not have to wonder how all this had come about; only Aladdin's possession of the enchanted lamp could have achieved this success for him. The knowledge filled the sorcerer with a murderous rage. Cursing the day he set eyes on the boy, the sorcerer swore an oath that he would destroy him. With the greatest haste, he left his own country. Traveling both day and night, he finally arrived in the sultan's capital.

The sorcerer secured a room in an inn, and then set out into the busy streets to learn what he could of Aladdin. This was not difficult, for everywhere he walked there was talk of nothing but Aladdin and his magnificence. People spoke of his generosity and bravery, and his palace was called the eighth wonder of the world. At last the sorcerer stopped one of the speakers.

"Excuse me, sir. Can you tell me of whom you speak?" he inquired pleasantly.

"You must be a stranger, my friend, if you do not know," said the man. "But no matter, surely you have heard of Prince Aladdin. He is known for miles around as the hero of our country and the kindest man who has ever lived. If you are stopping here, even for a short while, I urge you to at least see his palace before you leave."

"I would very much like to do just that," replied the sorcerer with a grim smile. "Would you be so kind as to direct me to it?"

The man gladly obliged by taking the sorcerer's arm and personally escorting him to the palace. As he did, he talked endlessly of Aladdin's glory till the sorcerer thought he would go mad with jealousy. After seeing the palace for himself, any doubt of the cause for Aladdin's prosperity was dispelled. No one but the great genie of the lamp could have built such a structure.

Flamed by envy, the magician plotted. "I must dig a grave for this Aladdin, who could not even earn the bread he ate before I met him. A grave, this time, from which he will never escape."

Alone in his room, the sorcerer cast his divining sands once more. He was delighted to learn that the lamp was in the palace and that Aladdin was away on a hunting trip. "It will be easier than I imagined to get what should always have been mine," he said to himself.

He went off to the nearest coppersmith and entered the shop. "I will pay you handsomely if you will make me a dozen copper lamps as quickly as possible. I am in a great hurry, and if you cannot do it immediately, I shall go elsewhere."

The coppersmith worked quickly and delivered the lamps before the end of the week. Without even looking over the workmanship, the sorcerer paid the price and sent the man on his way. He put the new lamps into a large basket and, after disguising himself as a peddler, he went out into the streets shouting, "New lamps for old! New lamps for old!"

People laughed as he passed, and some willingly brought him their battered lamps for shiny new ones. As he approached Aladdin's palace he began to shout louder and louder, "New lamps for old! New lamps for old!"

By now the street children followed after the funny peddler and echoed his words, "New lamps for old! New lamps for old!" over and over again till the square rang out with their chanting voices.

One of Princess Badoura's ladies-in-waiting heard the shouting and could not help laughing when she saw the cause of all the noise. "Your Highness, there is a madman outside our window offering brand-new copper lamps for old ones."

Badoura joined her at the window, and they both laughed at the foolish peddler. "My dear girl," said the princess, "we must find an old lamp to give to this foolish man at once. Come, help me find one."

The young women ran through the palace, enlisting whomever they encountered to help them. Servants and fine ladies joined in the search, everyone running and laughing from one room to the other until a servant girl remembered having seen an old lamp on the uppermost shelf off in a darkened corner of her master's room. Thinking the lamp held no particular value, she quickly went off to fetch it for her mistress. But it was the enchanted lamp! Aladdin had forgotten to lock it up before he left to go hunting, and no one in the palace, not even Badoura, knew of its powers.

"Here, Your Highness! Here!" she cried. "Here is an old lamp that certainly deserves to be replaced."

The princess took it from her and, without another thought, called to the peddler from her window, "Are you in earnest? Will you exchange this old lamp for one of your new ones?"

The sorcerer's palms sweated as he answered, "Yes, Your Royal Highness. Yes, indeed! *Old lamps for new!*"

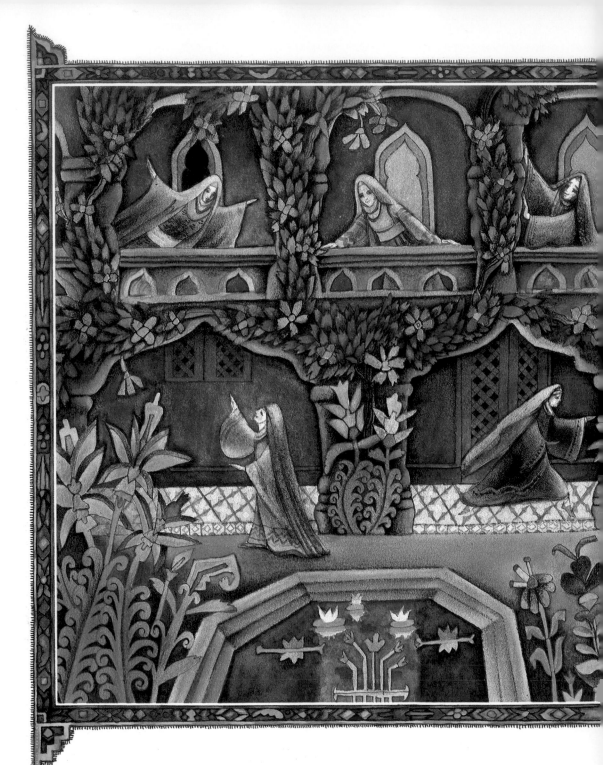

The sorcerer's palms sweated as he answered, "Yes, Your Royal Highness. Yes, indeed! Old lamps for new!"

"Then take this one," said the princess and, stifling a laugh, she tossed the precious lamp to him.

Down, down, down it fell, until it dropped into the sorcerer's eager hands. One of the princess's servants hurried to the street to receive a new shiny copper lamp from the peddler. She examined the new lamp and, seeing that it was quite perfect, she rushed back to her mistress. Badoura took it from her and, finding that it was really new, she burst out laughing with the others at the old man's folly.

Clasping the enchanted lamp to his breast, the sorcerer flung the basket filled with lamps at the mocking crowd that surrounded him. Then, quick as lightning, he broke through the circle of onlookers and ran.

He ran on and on till he reached a secluded spot outside the city. There he tried to calm his pounding heart as he waited for night to fall. At last, evening came, and in utter darkness, the sorcerer drew out the lamp. The sky as he looked toward the city was draped in black clouds, intensely black, meeting a black horizon—except for one slight rent of deep crimson which stretched westward behind the ancient city walls like a lake of blood. He rubbed the lamp once, twice, three times and held his breath. Suddenly flaming red smoke burst from the lamp, and its monstrous genie appeared before him.

"Master of the Lamp, I, who serve its owner, have heard your summons. Command and I shall obey," announced the genie.

"Slave of the Lamp," ordered the sorcerer in a shrill voice. "You who see everything and know all, hear me! I command you to transport me, along with Aladdin's palace and all it contains, to my native land. See that you set us close to where my tower stands."

"I hear and will obey. In a blink of your eyes, Master, you will be there."

There was a rumble of thunder, and at once all that had been ordered was done. Now the sorcerer possessed everything Aladdin had owned and loved.

*T*he next morning, the sultan woke early and, as was his custom, went to his window to gaze out at his daughter's beautiful palace. All was barren; a huge black hole lay gaping where the palace had stood just the day before.

The sultan gasped in horror; he could not bring himself to believe what he saw. Taking water from his basin, he splashed his face several times in the hope that he was dreaming some terrible nightmare and that this would wake him. He returned to the window, but again he beheld the same ghastly sight. It could not be and yet it was: The palace had vanished. The great sultan began to weep. The light of his life, his dearest child, was gone; he did not know where or how to find her.

He shouted to have the grand vizier brought to him immediately. The vizier hurried in, and when he saw the sultan's grief-stricken face, he begged to know the reason.

"Look out my window and tell me what, if anything, you see of my child's palace," cried the sultan, still weeping.

The vizier walked to the window and looked out. But it was what he did not see that caused the minister to stare in silence at the vast emptiness before him.

"And now, do you still wonder at my grief?" asked the sultan.

The sultan's words brought the minister back to attention. "Majesty, the answer to this horrible mystery can only come from one person," replied the vizier. "I told you, *warned you*, Your Highness, not to trust this Aladdin. I feared that something of this kind would happen sooner or later. It could only have been magic that created what he appeared to possess. Evil magic! And now it has turned to destruction."

"Where is Aladdin?" shouted the sultan in a boiling rage.

"Hunting, Sire. Or so he said. Already he has been gone some three days," replied the minister.

"Call out my troops at once to find him. Tell them I want the villain dragged to me in chains this very day, or they will feel the sting of my sword," ordered the sultan.

Officers and guards rode out immediately. When they found Aladdin, they drew their swords, but averted their eyes in embarrassment as they said, "Forgive us, beloved commander. We are under orders from the sultan himself to bring you back to his palace in chains."

Aladdin could not imagine what had happened, but he did not resist. "Good friends, can you not tell me the reason for such an order?"

"Commander, we do not know ourselves," they answered. "But if we disobey, we have been told we shall forfeit our own lives."

"Then you must carry out your orders," said Aladdin as he handed them his unsheathed sword.

They bound him, taking pains with the doing of the thing, and their hearts were filled with shame. Unhorsed and chained, Aladdin was dragged back to the city. The citizens wept as they saw him pass in such disgrace. By now there was not a person who did not know that Aladdin's palace had vanished, but their love for their hero prevented them from thinking ill of him. They feared that to see him so treated could only mean that he was to be executed.

At the sight of the troops and their prisoner, the sultan, without even facing Aladdin, gave orders to the executioner to have the cap-

. . . the sultan, without even facing Aladdin, gave orders to the executioner to have the captive's head cut off.

tive's head cut off. But the people came out of their homes and out of their shops to surround the palace. They pounded on the palace gates, shouting that if one hair on Aladdin's head was harmed, they would tear down the gates and destroy the king.

"Your Majesty," cautioned the frightened vizier. "Your order will bring down the wrath of your people on all of us. I fear your subjects love Aladdin more than any of us realized."

While this was going on, the executioner prepared for the beheading. Soon his sharp saber was poised over Aladdin's neck as he looked toward the sultan for the signal. Aladdin knelt in the public square, head bowed, chained and blindfolded, waiting for the executioner's saber to drop upon him.

Already the citizens were storming the palace. Men were climbing the locked gates, and the guards did not have the heart to stop them. Fear for his own life abated the sultan's anger just in time. He ordered the executioner to halt and sent word to his people that Aladdin had been pardoned.

But to the grand vizier, he whispered, "This villain Aladdin shall be spared for the moment. But I assure you, it is just *for the moment*."

Freed from his chains, Aladdin went to the sultan. "Majesty, I am ignorant of the charge that has been brought against me. Please, I beg of you, tell me what I have done to warrant your anger?"

"Liar!" shouted the sultan, with a grim face. "Do you dare to feign ignorance of your crime? Tell me then, where is my daughter?"

"Why, Sire," exclaimed the bewildered Aladdin, "I imagine she is in our palace, where I bade her farewell some three days ago."

"Scoundrel, if the crowd had not stayed my hand you would have gotten the executioner's sword, which you sorely deserve. Look out the window, and tell me where your palace is!"

Aladdin felt he was living through a nightmare. Shaking his head in confusion, he walked to the window and looked out. He saw nothing but desolation where his magnificent palace had once stood. Uttering a cry of alarm, he turned back to the sultan, pale as death.

"What, did you not see it, then?" the sultan shouted, sarcastically.

"Now, perhaps you will tell me where my daughter is, my dearest treasure in life, my only child!"

"Great King," replied Aladdin, "I swear on my life I know nothing of these events."

"Your life, indeed. I have spared it momentarily, so that you will investigate this mystery and find my daughter for me. Do not fail. Or I shall have your head in the bargain."

"Give me but forty days to search for her. I shall uncover the answers, or I will take my own life and save you the trouble. I would rather die than live without her in any case."

"Very well, I grant you forty days. But should you have a change of heart about your precious life, do not try to escape me. Make no mistake that I will be lax in this, for I will find you in whatever part of the world you choose to hide, even if it costs me my own life and kingdom in the doing."

The people cheered to see Aladdin leave the palace free again. But had they spoken to him, they would have found their hero a changed man. His mind was clouded and confused, and those who rejoiced at his release would have deeply pitied him had they known what was in his heart. For two days he wandered aimlessly, asking whomever he encountered if they knew anything of the whereabouts of his palace. Those who heard his questions shook their heads in dismay and walked away thinking he had lost his mind. Loyal friends brought him food and offered him shelter, but Aladdin refused them all, for he was too sick at heart to eat or sleep. At last he drifted out of the city, wanting only solitude to shield him from the probing eyes and kindness of those who loved him.

There in the desert surrounded by the arid sand, he thought to take his own life; his spirit was broken and all hope of finding Badoura seemed out of reach. He wept till there were no more tears to shed. Exhausted, he took water from his leather drinking bag and washed his tearstained face and grimy hands. As he did, he rubbed the rings he wore upon his fingers. One in particular was the very ring the sorcerer had given him so very long ago, for protection. Suddenly, the genie of the ring appeared in a cloud of green smoke.

"Good Master, it has been years since you summoned me. How can I serve you?" asked the genie of the ring.

In the face of his profound calamity, Aladdin was more than pleasantly surprised to see this familiar apparition. Hope sprang anew as he spoke in a voice filled with emotion. "Save my poor life, genie, as you already have once before. Return to me my dearest Badoura and the palace we shared together."

"What you ask is not of my realm, Good Master, and so it is impossible. I cannot go against the great genie of the lamp. He is one thousand and one times stronger than I. He removed the palace from where it stood. And it is solely by his power that the palace and all who abide in it can be restored to you."

"Very well," said Aladdin, disappointed but not yet defeated. "By the power of the ring, transport me to that place where the palace stands and set me down below Badoura's windows."

The words were no sooner out of Aladdin's mouth than the genie carried him, light as a feather, through clouds, space and miles of vast distance to North Africa and the country of Morocco. The genie placed him beneath the princess's windows and then left him.

It was darkest night, yet there in the transparent deep green shadows, he saw the palace. Surrounding and overhanging the site was a towering forest of centuries-old cedars, green oaks and pines. It seemed to him as he looked upon the faintly glowing image of the palace that it had always stood there within its wooded enclosure. Under the shadows of these ancient trees, Aladdin huddled and waited for the first rays of morning. His heart was lighter than it had been for some time. He was confident that somehow he would see his wife again, and for now this was all that mattered. Afterward, he would find the strength and wit to do whatever was necessary, but for the moment he could wait patiently and rest for the first time in many days.

Dawn came early. Bars of sunshine fell through the branches

above, across the dense tapestry of blue, yellow and crimson flowers that glowed so richly upon their dark green ground. Deep in this wild valley, buried among the shadows of tall old trees, Aladdin could now and then catch a glimpse of sparkling blue water. Looking back at the palace, he heard the drowsy calls of strange birds mingled with the songs of the exotic birds in Badoura's private garden.

While he waited for signs of stirring from her bedchamber, he went in search of the stream to drink and refresh himself. He followed a path carpeted with pink blossoms and smiled as he watched monkeys scurrying overhead from tree to tree. But at last he heard the movements of servants and his wife's own clear voice.

Here, in this natural paradise, Badoura was miserable. Since she had been abducted, she was forced to endure a visit from the hateful sorcerer once a day. He wanted her to love him, but she treated him so harshly that he dared not stay longer than a short while. The rest of the time he kept to his own tower close by. This morning, the princess was alone with her servants.

Aladdin threw a pebble at her window, hoping to attract her attention. As the princess was dressing, a servant girl, startled by the sound against the glass, looked out. The sight of Aladdin caused the girl to draw in her breath and gasp.

"Whatever is the matter?" asked the princess.

"Your Highness, my master, Aladdin, stands outside this very window," the girl answered.

Badoura rushed past her to see for herself. "If only you speak the truth," she cried.

At the sight of her husband, Badoura flung open the window and called to him, "Dearest Aladdin, I had almost given up hope of seeing you again. Quickly, my love, come through the garden; I will have the gates unlocked immediately."

In moments they were in each others' arms, laughing and crying with joy. At last, Aladdin took Badoura's hand and had her sit beside him.

... *Badoura flung open the window and called to him, "Dearest Aladdin, I had almost given up hope of seeing you again."*

"We must act quickly, now that I've found you. First, tell me what if anything, you know of an old lamp I kept on the uppermost shelf in my chamber."

"Oh, I feared that lamp had something to do with our misery. The day I gave it away, our troubles began." Badoura proceeded to tell Aladdin everything that had taken place from the minute she set eyes upon the peddler with the new copper lamps. "The very next morning, we awoke to find ourselves here in this foreign country. The man who had pretended to be a peddler came to me and said that his magic and the lamp's power had accomplished the deed. He told us we were in his power and that we would never escape."

"Then he has tricked us very cleverly indeed. Do not blame yourself," said Aladdin when Badoura began to apologize. "I never told you the value of that enchanted lamp, so how in the world were you to know that our happiness depended on it? Dry your eyes, my love. Between us, we must come up with a plan to get that precious lamp back from the sorcerer."

"The wretch comes to visit me every afternoon at four. Over and over he tells me that you are dead and that I should forget you. He thinks that if I come to believe him, I will one day consent to be his wife. The lamp you speak of is always with him; it hangs from a sash tied around his waist."

Aladdin shook his head. "But if it is always with him, how shall I ever get it?"

"Leave that to me. Since it was I who lost your lamp for you, let me try to get it back without your risking your life," said Badoura.

Aladdin tried to dissuade her, pointing out the danger she would face. But she spoke courageously and insisted that he let her try.

"He attempts to be very gracious to me in the hope that he will win my heart. But he has never heard me speak a kind word to him. Today this will change. You must hide yourself; he must not suspect that you are here, or all will be lost. I will call you if I need you. Please do as I ask, and I promise I will not fail."

Aladdin's protests did him no good, and finally the force of her argument made him agree to her wishes. After he was put in a safe place to wait, the princess called her maids.

"Listen to me. I intend to welcome that old sorcerer, dressed in my loveliest robes. Help me to get ready. Everything must be perfect. Fetch wine and good things to eat; I wish to have prepared a delicate light supper for two. There must be candles and lamps lighted. Bring armfuls of jasmine from the garden and burn incense of sandalwood for this romantic evening. And once he arrives, I wish no one to disturb us."

When she was alone, the princess went to her bed and pulled from under it a small trunk. She took from it a phial, which she then quickly hid away in her robes.

The Moroccan arrived promptly at four o'clock and was greeted with a warm welcome from the smiling princess. She invited him to dine with her, saying she had considered all he had told her and finally decided that Aladdin was indeed dead.

"You are my only friend in the world," she said, smiling beautifully at the sorcerer. "Forgive me for my unkind words in the past. Please understand it was my grief at losing my husband that caused me to behave so cruelly toward you. I deeply regret it and wish to make it up to you. Stay with me, so that we may dine together tonight."

The sorcerer was thrilled at this turn of events. The princess's beauty beguiled him; now that he possessed the enchanted lamp, he wished to own Badoura as well. He agreed happily to her offer and settled himself down for a pleasant evening.

But no sooner had the princess seen that he was willing than she took his gnarled hand in hers, saying, "There is a custom in my country. I do not know if you have the same here, but I think you will agree that it is charming, nonetheless. When we make friends with someone from a foreign land, we ask that we exchange wines from each other's countries at dinner. Do you mind? I wish to drink the wine of Morocco this evening if you will indulge me."

The sorcerer was so enchanted . . . he did not hesitate, but took the glass from her outstretched hand and gulped it down.

The sorcerer was only too eager to oblige her, so he hurried off again to his own wine cellars to bring her a large beaker of his very best wine. While he was about it, Badoura took from her pocket the phial she had hidden. She poured the contents into the carafe of wine on the dining table and seated herself again to wait for the sorcerer.

He returned quickly with the wine and placed it beside the other carafe.

"Now we must have a toast as it is done in my humble country with you drinking my wine from my glass and me drinking yours," said the princess as she poured the wines into their glasses, one from his bottle for her and the other for him from her own.

Before handing him the glass, she caressed it gracefully and then kissed the edge of the rim. The sorcerer was so enchanted by her gestures and words that he did not hesitate, but took the glass from her outstretched hand and gulped it down. He turned to look at her and started to say something, but fell from his seat in a deathlike sleep.

Badoura pulled herself up, and her trembling hand went to her mouth as she watched him fall. Then she cried out to her servants to fetch Aladdin.

He came rushing into the room, saw the stricken sorcerer lying where he had fallen and took Badoura into his arms.

"He is drugged. I have given him a heavy dose of a sleeping potion. Do with him what you feel is best; the lamp still remains attached to his sash."

Aladdin pulled his dagger out to take revenge on the sorcerer, but found he could not do it. Shaking his head, he turned to his wife.

"I have never killed a man except in war. Now faced with killing this defenseless villain, I find I do not have the stomach for murder. I cannot kill him even if he does deserve it."

Instead, Aladdin took up the lamp from the sorcerer's belt and rubbed it three times. At once, the genie of the wonderful lamp appeared in a cloud of bright red smoke.

"Master, I am here to do your bidding. Ask and I shall obey," said the genie, bowing from the waist.

"Very good," said Aladdin. "Take this creature to the depths of the cavern of treasures and see to it that he is imprisoned in black stone. Once it was what he hoped for me; now he shall endure it for all the grief he has caused me and my wife. When this is done, return to me quickly; there is still one more thing I will need you to do."

In seconds both the genie and the unconscious sorcerer had vanished into thin air. Aladdin and Badoura had only a little time to exchange words before the genie of the enchanted lamp returned.

"What more can I do for you, Master?" asked the genie.

"Take us and our palace back to the place it stood before you were ordered to remove it."

In a flash of lightning, the deed was done. Aladdin and Badoura were settled once more in their own country, believing themselves safe at last from the horrid sorcerer.

Since the disappearance of his daughter, the sultan had been inconsolable. He wept day and night over the loss of his only child. From time to time, he returned to the window and gazed out at the spot where her palace had once stood.

On this particular morning, he woke as usual after a miserable night of troubling thoughts about Badoura's dangerous fate. He rose and walked to the window, shaking his head and cursing himself for ever trusting Aladdin. He saw a building—the very palace that had disappeared!

Taking heed of nothing else, he set out at once for the dwelling. Badoura and Aladdin saw him approaching and ran out to meet him. The sultan caught his daughter in his arms like a bouquet of the rarest blossoms and hugged her with relief. Then he begged to know if she was well and to be told what had happened.

Badoura described to her father the events that had taken place. The sultan then stretched out his arms to Aladdin and embraced him.

"Forgive me," said the king. "In my misery, I blamed you unjustly for this misfortune. The loss of my child made me half-crazed with grief. Now I must beg your pardon and thank you for restoring her to me."

"Your Majesty, you have done me no wrong," said Aladdin graciously. "We are all safe now that that wicked sorcerer is out of our sight forever."

The capital was decorated for a grand celebration. A public festival was declared, and the sultan sent out heralds to proclaim a holiday in honor of the return of the princess and her husband. All was well —or so it seemed.

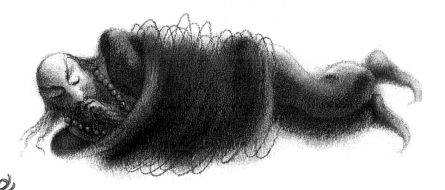

For a while Aladdin and the princess lived happily and peace-
fully together, thinking themselves free from the sorcerer.

The genie of the lamp had carried away the unconscious sorcerer
to the cavern of treasures as he had been instructed. He placed the
magician in one of the enchanted rooms of gold. At the instant the
body touched the floor, the enchantment began. A sinister web, like
spun black gold, wound round and round him. The genie watched as
the thick layers of filament slowly merged and hardened, encasing
the sleeping figure in smooth impenetrable black stone. Believing his
task accomplished, the genie hastened to his master to fulfill the next
request.

Suspended in timelessness, the sorcerer slept on and on. When he
did awaken from the deadening sleep, he discovered he was sealed in
stone. His heart almost died within him as he faced the unspeakable
horror. In a panic, he struggled wildly to force his way out without
success. Magic, he told himself frantically, was the only possibility.
But was his magic potent enough?

Drawing from his great knowledge of magical incantations, three
times he attempted to free himself and three times he failed. Hatred
for Aladdin fortified him; he would not give up, and he tried again.
The force of the next spell sent a tremor through the stone. Imper-

ceptible cracks lined its surface. Bit by bit these cracks deepened, splitting the dense stone until suddenly it burst apart. Another powerful spell freed him from the chamber, and at last he stood in the open to breathe the fresh night air.

Revenge was still in his heart. His surprising release had not dulled his hatred of Aladdin. Now the regaining of the lamp was only secondary to his passionate desire to destroy the young man. But having once possessed the powers of the enchanted lamp, he was not going to forget that, either. Once more, the sorcerer returned to the city where he knew he would find his enemy. He did not hurry; rather, he traveled at an easy pace, scheming and plotting as he went.

In due time he reached the capital and took up lodgings in the district, causing no attention to be brought to himself. He watched and plotted, waiting for the right moment to strike.

There was a holy woman, a healer called Fatima, who was renowned in the area for her miraculous cures. She came to the city only twice a month. The rest of the time she devoted herself to prayer and abstinence in her hermit's shelter far from town. When the people of the city saw her arrive on one of these special visits, they rushed to her, crowding around her, begging for a blessing or to be healed by her holy hands. She never failed to heal those who asked, taking nothing in return. Because of this, the people revered her and called her a saint.

There was not a soul who did not know of her miracles, and soon the sorcerer learned of her. When he did, an idea came to him. He marked her movements, and on the day of one of her visits, he followed Fatima as she left the town. Reaching her hermit's hut in the woods, the good woman entered, never suspecting that the sorcerer was not far behind.

When he assured himself that there was no one to protect her, he burst in and attacked the defenseless woman. Holding a knife to her throat, the sorcerer threatened her life, saying that if she helped him to disguise himself to look like her, he would not kill her.

The poor, frightened woman agreed. She gave him clothes, veils

. . . the good woman entered, never suspecting that the sorcerer was not far behind.

and sacred beads. Adorned in this holy costume, the sorcerer preened before the glass, fixing his eyes with a dove-like expression. He was convinced that he and Fatima could not now be told apart. Then the dove's eyes were gone, and the serpent's eyes returned to look savagely upon the healer.

The sorcerer's slender hands sprang on Fatima's throat, and his gnarled knuckles, hard and sharp, were pressed against her jawbone as he shook her. His face was black as night, with two red, fiery eyes glaring out. The attack was so violent that she was thrown off balance against the wall. Stunned, Fatima fell to the floor in a faint; swiftly, the sorcerer plunged his dagger into her till she was dead.

He washed her blood from his hands and then set out to pay a second visit to the town. When he arrived the people thronged to him, thinking he was indeed their beloved Fatima. The sorcerer did what he remembered seeing the healer do to those who pleaded for her blessings. Surrounded by the adoring crowd, the impostor made his way toward the square where Aladdin's palace stood.

The princess saw holy Fatima in the streets and yearned to have her come into the palace to visit. She called one of her servants and sent him out to ask the healer if she would agree to enter the palace.

The servant returned with the disguised sorcerer. The impostor bowed low and in a soft voice offered a prayer for the princess's continuing life and health. Badoura helped the holy woman to rise and made her follow so that they could sit undisturbed in the private garden.

"For so long, I have hoped to meet you," said the princess. "It has been my wish that you would stay with us, here in my home. If you would agree, I could have a chance to learn from you and follow your good example. Won't you say yes?"

The invitation was just what the sorcerer had hoped for, but he feigned hesitation nonetheless rather than appear too eager.

Fixing his eyes with an icy stare on the princess, he said tranquilly, "Your Royal Highness, I thank you for the great honor you pay me. But I am a humble woman. I make my home, such as it is, in a tiny hut in the woods where I can pray in solitude. I could not dwell in your grand palace."

The princess saw that fleeting look. It startled her though she told herself it was only the light.

"But surely, holy Fatima, if I promised that you would have utter privacy? You should have a quiet room all to yourself where no one would disturb you. Please reconsider. It would mean so much to me if you would agree, even for just a little while," pleaded the princess.

"How can I refuse, Your Majesty?" said the crafty sorcerer, with a faint gleam of his unpleasant smile safely concealed beneath his veil. Sure that the princess was totally misled, he continued, "But I must ask that I be allowed to remain in my room the better part of each day. I eat very little; a bit of bread and water is all I require, for fasting is part of my devotional duties. This simple food I must eat alone, and you must promise that no one will intrude upon me."

The sorcerer's major fear was that if he were to share his meals with the rest of the household, he would be forced to reveal who he really was when he lifted his veil to eat.

The princess willingly agreed to these simple terms, thinking all the more what a sincerely devout person Fatima was. "Of course, all you ask, little as it is, shall be done. Now come, I will show you the palace, and then after that you shall choose your rooms."

Badoura showed the disguised sorcerer through every inch of the palace, and at each marvel he complimented its beauty. When they reached the jeweled dome, the false Fatima stopped and took the princess's hand.

"This is a wonder beyond compare, Your Majesty. But, nonetheless, it lacks one thing. Will you forgive my boldness if I say so?" he asked in the same silken tone.

"By all means, please tell me. It is your wisdom and clear insight that I wish you to share with me. Speak," urged the princess.

"Very well, then you must understand that it is my inner eye, my mind's vision, that tells me what must be placed in the center of this exquisite dome. It is a message to me from the heavens above, you see. A roc's egg must come to hang from the uppermost point at the ceiling of the dome. Only then will the palace be utterly complete."

"But what is this animal you speak of? I know nothing of it," said the bewildered princess.

"Oh, Your Highness! It is a fabulous white bird of enormous size with such strength that it can carry an elephant in its talons. A roc's egg is truly the eighth wonder of the world, its beauty is impossible to describe, and because of this, one must hang from your wonderful dome," explained the impostor.

"How could one be found?" asked the princess, eagerly.

"My Lady, legend tells us these birds are only found in the distant mountains of Kif," said the sorcerer, as he shook his veiled head sadly. "But certainly, the builder of this incredible dome could find such an egg!"

The princess's mind was filled with the holy woman's words as she led her to her rooms.

"There, there, My Royal Princess. Do not trouble yourself with my fancies. Perhaps my vision was mistaken. . . . If you fear that a roc's egg cannot be gotten, I'm sure no harm will come to your household," said the sorcerer with grave significance.

There was the suspicion of a sneer—not in his tone, not necessarily in his words—but somehow a suspicion stung Badoura like the sharpened point of a dagger.

"Harm!" she cried. "You said nothing of harm before this. Please tell me everything."

"My inner eye tells me that misfortune has in the past plagued you. Forgive me, dare I go on?" asked the clever sorcerer.

"Yes, yes. It is true. Please go on."

"Well then, my vision—but, mind you, it was none too clear—warns that if a roc's egg, which holds great good luck, is not placed where I told you, misfortune may strike again. Of course, I may be mistaken," replied the sorcerer as he eyed the trusting princess.

"No, I am told you are *never* mistaken when making a prophecy. Oh, thank goodness you have come to us, most blessed Fatima. You did right to tell me. I will see to it at once." And with that the princess bade the holy woman a comfortable stay and hurried away to find Aladdin.

Badoura found him in his own chamber, and when he turned to greet her, he could not help but see that she was deeply troubled. Alarmed, Aladdin immediately asked for the reason.

"It is nothing really, my love. But I have been told that the possession of a roc's egg gives great good fortune. Perhaps in light of our past misfortune, it would be well if we had one hanging from the domed ceiling."

"Badoura, you have never asked for anything from me before. If you wish to own a roc's egg, you shall have it," said Aladdin, kissing the top of her head affectionately.

After Badoura left him, Aladdin took up the lamp and rubbed it three times. The genie of the enchanted lamp appeared instantly in a cloud of red smoke. He bowed low and asked, "Master, what is your desire?"

"Good genie, I wish for a roc's egg to hang from the dome of the palace."

The genie roared like a demon, glaring at Aladdin savagely. "Ungrateful fool," he shouted. "Is what I have given you for the asking not enough to satisfy you? Must you also ask that I bring you my mistress to hang like an ornament from your ceiling to amuse you? *She* who lives within the shelter of the mighty roc's egg, the mother of all genies!

"If I didn't know that you had been tricked into making this blasphemous request, I would burn you and everything else in this palace and scatter the ashes to the four corners of the world. Ignorant human, it is the Moroccan sorcerer himself who has put your wife up to this. He hides in the palace now, disguised as a holy woman whom he has already killed. And he would do the same to you, if he

The genie roared like a demon, glaring at Aladdin savagely.
"Ungrateful fool," he shouted.

didn't think that by your asking such a thing from me I would do his work for him. I will forgive this insult, but I will not do what you bid me!" With that, the genie vanished in a clap of thunder.

Pale and shaken, Aladdin sat down. But he soon recovered and made up his mind what he must do next.

Holding his head, Aladdin returned to his wife and complained of a severe headache that was making him quite ill. Badoura soothed him and promised she would see that he felt better.

"As luck would have it, I have invited the healer, holy Fatima, to stay with us. I shall call her at once; she will cure you," said Badoura.

"That would be wonderful," replied Aladdin. "Please show her in, for I am really dizzy with pain."

Soon the Moroccan entered, his head bowed and his face concealed by his veil. Aladdin got up and welcomed the pretender.

"Mistress, I beg of you, place your healing hands on my head. I have a fierce pain that I am told only you can cure."

The sorcerer could hardly contain his eagerness at the invitation to be close enough to the stricken Aladdin to slay him. He came up behind Aladdin, laying one hand on his head as he pulled his dagger from beneath his robes.

But Aladdin was poised for the attack. "Old villain!" he exclaimed, starting up with sudden force. He caught the sorcerer's hand and pulled the dagger from him, thrusting it into the assassin's heart.

"What have you done?" Badoura screamed. "How could you kill this poor holy woman? We will be cursed forever."

Aladdin took the veil from the sorcerer's face. "See for yourself who this really is. *This* is the man who murdered Fatima, not I. He disguised himself as her to do the same to me. But at last we are free of him."

"Aladdin, this is the second time I have thrown you into danger," said Badoura as she put her arms around him.

"Hush, it is all the fault of this sorcerer, and we are now finished with him. As for danger, I would gladly risk my life for one loving glance from you."

"Do you really love me so much?" asked the princess.
"More than I can ever say," he told her.

At last they were able to live happily, and no other danger touched them. From Aladdin and Badoura's loving union, sons and daughters were born who grew to be great kings and queens. The sultan and Aladdin's mother delighted in watching their grand-children and great-grandchildren grow and prosper. In old age, the sultan gave the kingdom to his daughter and her husband, and they reigned justly.

This book was set in 12-point Palatino.
The text was composed by Maryland Linotype
Composition Co., Inc.
Printing was done by Princeton Polychrome Press.
Binding was done by A. Horowitz & Sons.
Typography and binding design by
Gerald McDermott and Ellen Friedman.
The illustrations were rendered in watercolor
and pastel pencil on bristol board.